Adventures with Bobbie Bee

Bee Medicine

Written by Megan McFarlane and Illustrated by Suzie Ramsay

To order additional copies of this book, contact:
Xlibris
AU TFN: 1 800 844 927 (Toll Free inside Australia)
AU Local: 02 8310 8187 (+61 2 8310 8187 from outside Australia)
www.xlibris.com.au
Orders@Xlibris.com.au

| ISBN: | Softcover | 979-8-3694-9281-9 |
| | EBook | 979-8-3694-9282-6 |

Library of Congress Control Number: 2023914236

Print information available on the last page

Rev. date: 09/15/2023

This book belongs to:

_____

Foreword

I would like to honour my parents with this book. Dad, whose nick name is Macca and my Mother Pattie, who are both characters in the *Adventures with Bobbie Bee* series of books as the Farmer and Farmers' wife.

Sunny Downs was the farm I grew up on and I'm so grateful to my parents for creating a magical home and place for us to live. It has invested heavily in the inspirational moments forged into my imagination as a child, to be able to create *Adventures with Bobbie Bee.*

I also dedicate this book to my five precious grandchildren; Matthew, Oliver, Jerry, Flynn, Levi and another "Bun in the Oven". They are a part of the creativity in writing this book. May they live to change the world.

Bobbie Bee Apiary and his family lived in the delightful little town called Beeville.

Their house was positioned on the highest point in town, right in the middle of the street called Blossom Place. Every day was busy and full of adventures for all the bees who lived in Beeville, especially in Blossom Place. It was known for having the highest-quality honey flow and the best bee products in the neighbourhood.

Beeville was situated on a farm called Sunny Downs. Macca the farmer and his wife, Pattie, were the humans who owned and worked the farm. They loved looking after the bees and rather enjoyed keeping them. They knew that the bees were very good for the environment and pollinated many different plants and crops. The bees worked tirelessly, creating the delightful, sticky golden-amber substance called honey. Macca and Pattie loved to package the great-tasting honey up into jars with a clever little label they had designed.

The mornings started very early for the bees, as everyone needed to be up out of bed, dressed, finished with breakfast, and off to tackle the day. Everyone in Beeville worked very hard collecting pollen, nectar, sap, and water. These were all the essential ingredients required to feed and run an efficient, well-organised hive.

Bobbie Bee enjoyed living with his family in a very large house called a three-stacker hive. He lived there with his mother, Betty; his dad, Flynn; and his sister, Tiffany.

The house was painted in three different colours, decoratively covered in a wild spray of beautiful flowers. The whole family loved their house, and it was very easy for them to spot it when returning home in flight from a very busy day.

Every morning Bobbie Bee's dad, Flynn Apiary, would announce in a very loud, proud, and fun-filled voice, "Remember, the early bee gets the honey!"

On this glorious morning, as Betty was making breakfast, her joyful voice loudly resonate throughout the hive. "Breakfast is the most important meal of the day."

Typically, breakfast included a combination of freshly baked bee bread and brightly coloured, magical-looking grains of pollen, all topped off with delicious blue gum nectar juice.

Bobbie Bee loved his mother's cooking and would always be the first one to the table to say, "Yummy!"

But on this particular morning, when he shuffled to the table, Betty noticed that Bobbie Bee was not his normal bright, happy, energy-filled self. He looked rather pale and not very well at all.

"Mum, my throat is all scratchy, and my nose is leaking," moaned Bobbie Bee as he wiped his runny nose on his sleeve.

Betty felt Bobbie Bee's forehead. "Mmmm, you feel very hot. I wonder where you could have picked this up from. Where have you been this week?"

Bobbie Bee shrugged. "I dunno."

Then Betty took a closer look at him. "What are these big brown spots I see?"

Tiffany and Flynn joined Bobbie Bee at the table, poured themselves huge bowls of pollen pellets, drowned them in nectar juice, and then scooped up mouthfuls with their spoons.

"You don't look so good, Bobbie Bee," Tiffany said between bites whilst giving Bobbie Bee a suspiciously knowing look. "Maybe you got sick from—"

"I don't think so," interrupted Bobbie Bee, staring at her intently.

"You should take him to see Dr. Drone, dear," said Flynn.

Betty grabbed Bobbie Bee's head, moving it back and forth while looking for spots on his neck. "You haven't even touched your breakfast; it's off to the doctor with you, my boy!"

"But, Mum, do I have to? Today's really important at school! We're doing football tryouts, and Coach Jensen is looking at putting me up to be the team captain. All my friends will be there, and if I don't go, I'll miss out on all the fun."

"Football will just have to wait," said Betty as she pushed a grumpy, reluctant Bobbie Bee out the hive door to fly him to the doctor.

At Dr. Drone's office, Betty noticed that Bobbie Bee's brown spots had swollen into larger lumpy spots. "This will not do; this will not do at all! Can you please help Bobbie Bee, Dr. Drone?" she said, looking very concerned.

"Mrs. Apiary, your son is in good hands," Dr. Drone said in a reassuring tone, holding her arm to try to calm her down. "Now, Bobbie Bee, let's have a look at you. Let me help you up onto my examination table; it's quite high for a little fellow such as yourself."

"They're so itchy," Bobbie Bee complained. Then he started to scratch profusely.

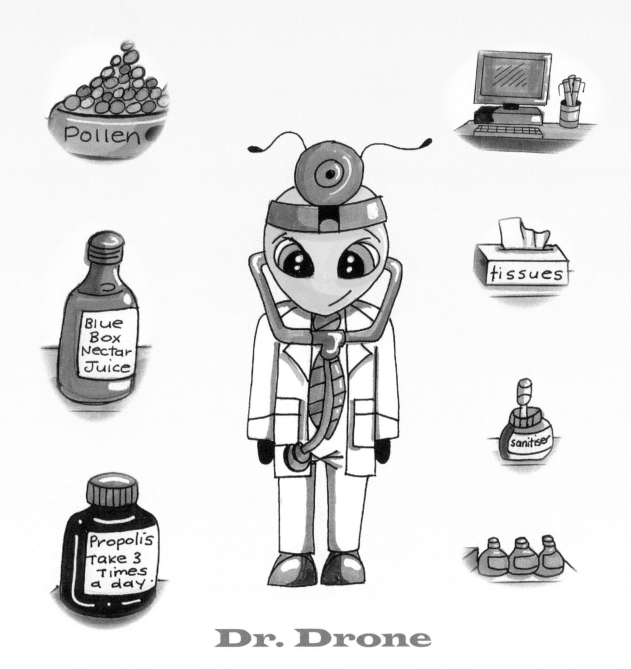

Dr. Drone

"Don't scratch; it will only make them worse," said Dr. Drone.

"I'm trying not to," Bobbie Bee groaned as he continued to scratch one and then another.

"Stop it, Bobbie Bee Apiary!" said Betty.

"Okay, okay, this won't take long," said Dr. Drone. "Now hold still, Bobbie Bee, while I take a careful look at you."

Then Dr. Drone carefully wiped one of the brown, itchy lumps with a swab and placed the slide under the microscope. "Hmm, very interesting," he said. He rubbed his chin again and frowned slightly.

"What's very interesting?" asked Betty, beginning to hover.

"Well, it appears that your son has a case of Varroa mites."

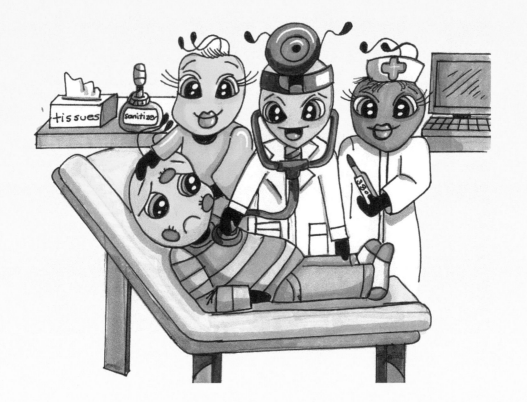

"Oh no! That's contagious, isn't it?" exclaimed Betty, shaking her head.

"Well, yes, but all will be okay if it's managed properly. For now, Bobbie Bee will need to stay at home and rest for two weeks while he's getting better." Dr. Drone flipped out his prescription tablet and proceeded to write.

Then he said, "Mrs Apiary, give Bobbie Bee ten spoons of propolis and five grains of pollen three times a day. This should deal with any pain and fever he may experience, and over the next ten days, he will gradually get better. Then bring Bobbie Bee back for a checkup to see whether we can

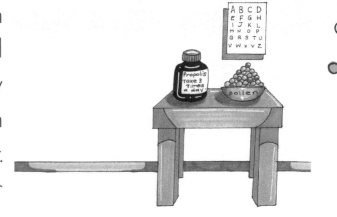

give him a full bill of health to go back to school."

Betty nodded, holding her forehead as though she had a painful headache.

Bobbie Bee was very frustrated at the instructions of the doctor, but Betty thanked the doctor and took a very itchy, grumpy, and whiny Bobbie Bee home.

Once there she said, "Into bed with you, Bobbie Bee. I'll bring you some of my famously delicious chicken soup; it should help you feel much better."

Being a good boy, Bobbie Bee dragged himself sluggishly into bed, and his mother brought him some chicken soup and medicine. When he had finished, Bobbie Bee lay down, stirring anxiously as he drifted off into a deep sleep where he dreamt about his previous week's adventures.

The dream began with Bobbie Bee and his two friends Oliver and Mattie playing near the duck pond.

"What's that?" yelled Bobbie Bee as a shadow passed overhead.

"It looked like something crashing into the mud near the tall reeds," Mattie said.

"Let's go check it out," Oliver answered.

Bobbie Bee hesitated. "But Mum said we should never go near the tall, boggy reeds. It's dangerous; we could get stuck in the mud—or worse."

"It'll be okay, and your mum will never know. We'll be back before you can say *sticky mud*," Oliver said.

So the three boys agreed, and they flew over to the reeds where they had seen something crash. As they got closer, they saw a helpless little girl bee covered in mud from head to toe and sinking quickly.

Bobby Bee, now forgetting about his reluctance, called out, "I'll save you!"

The boys flew down and helped pull her free from the muddy bog and took her over to a safer location on the bank of the duck pond.

The girl bee, in shock and crying, said, "I was lost, and a gust of wind blew me down into this muddy, boggy hole."

"It's okay; you're all safe now," Bobbie Bee said reassuringly. "What's your name?"

The cute bee was covered in mud and out of breath. She said, "I'm Amelia." She looked down at herself and shook her head. "Oh no, I'm wet, dirty, and lost! What am I gonna do? Mum won't be happy with me; I'll get into so much trouble."

Bobbie Bee noticed that Amelia had brown, lumpy spots all over her. "What are these?" he said awkwardly.

"I overheard the adults saying it was something called Varroa mites. Our whole hive got infected."

"Oh, so scary," Mattie said, making awkward faces, as if he wasn't taking her seriously. "Well, we better get you home. Where do you come from?"

"I'm from Orchard Box, on the Donaldsons' farm."

"Ah, that's ages away!" moaned Oliver.

Suddenly, two large boy bees came flying in and called out, "Amelia! We've been looking all over for you." Then, without warning, they nabbed Amelia and flew away.

The boys, now startled, looked towards the direction the other bees had flown and noticed Bobbie Bee's sister, Tiffany, hiding behind one of the duck pond reeds.

Bobbie Bee snapped out of his dream thinking about seeing Tiffany. He wondered about Amelia and what had happened to her. Being extremely tired, fever-ridden, and still quite itchy, he drifted back into a deep sleep and started to dream about what it would be like to live in Orchard Box and have Amelia as his friend. Bobbie Bee imagined jumping rope with her and their friends. All the children in his dream were chanting a rhyme to the jump rope rhythm, and it went like this:

Buzzy, fuzzy bees

bend at the knees!

Jump, jump, jump

higher than the trees!

Secrets sworn,

mystery born

at forbidden place—

windmill, reeds, and boggy space.

Watched her fall with a thud.

Save the girl from the mud!

Caught out the lie from sister spied.

If truth gets out, I'll be fried.

Suddenly, Bobbie Bee snapped out of his sleep in a cold sweat and wondered what would happen to him if his parents found out. He flew around his room trying to think of how to avoid being caught out. Then there was a *tap, tap, tap* on his window.

Bobbie Bee looked outside, and there was Oliver. He opened his window carefully so as not to make a noise. "What are you doing here?" he said.

"Just wanted to see what you were up to." Oliver was covered in brown lumps as well.

"Trying to get better, dude. I'm really annoyed that we missed the football tryouts, and now we are all stuck in bed. I'm also wondering whether my sister will tell on us when she gets back from her friend's place. She's staying at a friend's house while I'm sick. Maybe I should just tell my parents the truth about what happened."

Oliver furrowed his brow and looked into his eyes. "To be clear, Bobbie Bee, we won't be telling anybody about this. Will we?"

Bobbie Bee shook his head. "Maybe we should; we could have infected our whole hive."

Oliver leaned in towards Bobbie Bee. "We had a deal; you swore that you wouldn't tell a soul. We could get into so much trouble for this."

"I don't like lying, Oliver."

"But you *promised.*"

Bobbie Bee considered Oliver's words, and after a moment, he said, "I don't like it."

Then Oliver left frustrated. Just as Bobbie Bee was closing his window his mother came in.

"Bobbie Bee, what are you doing?" she demanded. "Why are you out of bed?"

"I was just getting some fresh air."

"Okay, well, back into bed. Come on." Betty placed her hand on his shoulder and escorted him back to bed.

Finally, when the ten days were up, Bobbie's mother took him back to the doctor's office, where he got the all-clear. The next day, back at school, he ran into the playground and was so excited to see all his friends.

Bobbie Bee's friends cautiously jumped back, and one of them said, "Whoa, bro, aren't you contagious? We heard you had Varroa mites."

"Yeah, but the doctor said I'm all better now."

Bobbie Bee's sister, Tiffany, was standing close by and listening. She piped up in a tattletale voice, "I followed you and saw you rescue the girl who crashed into the mud."

The boys went white as all the blood drained from their faces; then they all glared at Tiffany. The three boys looked at each other, and Mattie said, "I think you're dreaming, Tiffany; just be quiet."

"No, I'm not," said Tiffany. "I saw her fall out of the sky, and you three went and saved her near the windmill, where the boggy mud and tall reeds are. Then the two boy bees came and took her away. I'm going to tell Mum on you."

All the other kids who had been listening intently started teasing the three boys, saying, "Ooh, whose girlfriend is she?"

The boys denied it, shaking their heads. "What girl?" Oliver said.

At the end of the school day, Bobbie Bee was not looking forward to going home, as he knew that he would have to deal with his sister, who had been staying at her friend's place while he was sick. When he arrived home, he entered the kitchen and called out, "Mum I'm home! What's that amazing smell?

"It's a honeybee sting cake, which I made to celebrate your first day back at school."

"Awesome," said Bobbie Bee with a huge smile on his face. "My favourite!" Momentarily forgetting all about Tiffany, he ran to the table to sit and eat his yummy piece of cake.

Just then, Tiffany arrived home from school. She entered the room and immediately blurted out, "Muuum, Bobbie Bee went to the boggy tall reed place near the windmill."

Bobbie Bee gave his sister a harsh look.

"Did you go there, Bobbie Bee?" Betty asked in a stern voice. "Now, tell the truth."

Bobbie Bee swallowed very hard and nearly choked on the piece of cake he had stuffed into his mouth just prior to all the commotion.

Betty grabbed Bobbie Bee's plate. "No more cake for you until you tell the truth."

Bobbie Bee reached after his piece of cake as his mother took it away. Contemplating his options, he momentarily sat there in silence. Then, becoming flustered, he threw his arms up into the air. "We were all there." And he continued in a high-pitched voice, "Amelia was stuck in the mud; we had to save her, or she would have drowned."

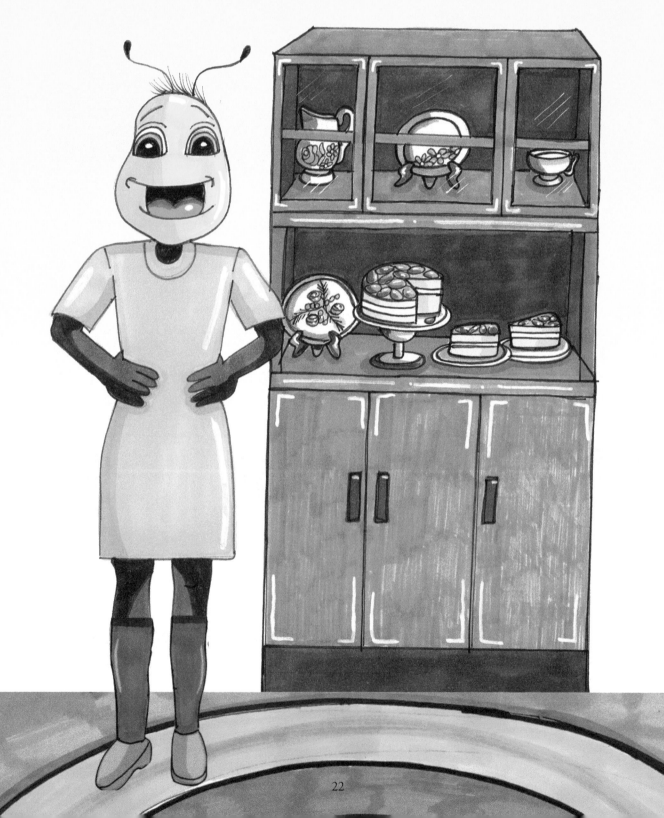

"Amelia? Who is Amelia? Why am I only hearing about this now? You know how dangerous that bog is; you should never go there without an adult." Then she glared at Tiffany. "What were *you* doing there?" Betty took away Tiffany's piece of cake as well. "You'll get your cake back when you decide to tell me the truth, young lady."

Tiffany's shoulders shrank into a hunched position. Her voice wavered when she said, "I followed the boys after school to see where they were going."

Betty put her hands on her hips. "Bobbie Bee, you endangered not only yourself and your two friends but your little sister as well—and you lied to me!"

"But, Mum, there was no time!"

"Not another word, Bobbie Bee. We'll talk to your father when he gets home."

Later that night around the dinner table, when all was told, Flynn expressed his feelings of disappointment and concern that both children had chosen to be dishonest. "You know both your mother and I love you deeply. I don't know what we would have done if something had happened to you."

Tears welled up in Betty's eyes, and she looked hurt and upset. "Why did you feel the need to lie to me?" she asked. "You know you can trust us to help you."

"I know, Mum," Bobbie Bee said with a sad look on his face. "I love you too, but everything moved so fast. I'm so sorry."

Flynn motioned everyone to come in for a group hug. "Now, remember—we are family. And what do families do?"

"We work things out together," everyone said in unison.

It was Bobbie Bee's bedtime, so Flynn and Betty said prayers with Bobbie Bee and tucked him into bed. As Bobbie Bee snuggled under the covers, he felt a sense of relief to have gotten this whole series of events off his chest. He came to the deep realisation that trust, truth, and love are the best medicine of all. Drifting off to sleep, he began to dream of Amelia and wondered whether he would ever see her again.

Printed in the USA
CPSIA information can be obtained
at www.ICGtesting.com
JSHW071123250124
55799JS00020B/441